Advance Praise

"*The Letter from Death* warns of the senseless killing in war and should inspire peace to protect the living."

Benjamin B. Ferencz, *Former Nuremberg war crimes prosecutor*

"… Lillian Moats' courageous tour de force invites us to see our own destructiveness, the world's human-created horrors, from death's point of view, as it sets the record straight before falling silent. Neither a terrifying force nor a gateway to justice, death protests against being used as history's bad guy and humanity's worst nightmare – warning humans against our addiction to war, agitating us to turn, while we still can, to face our real problems."

Ronald Aronson, *author of* Living without God: New Directions for Atheists, Agnostics, Secularists, and the Undecided

"*The Letter from Death* is exquisite – acutely imagined, well-crafted, vivid, simultaneously transcendent and focused. Who better than Death to explain the addiction of the death culture? Who better able to document the horror? What a book! It deserves a large, large audience."

William Ayers, *Distinguished Professor of Education, University of Illinois at Chicago*

ACTON MEMORIAL LIBRARY
486 Main St. Acton, MA 01720
(978) 929-6655

"I devoured this book. Lillian Moats brilliantly makes Death the narrator of a tour through hell and war, v   itself. … Filled with punch lines that mal   ie end of the book we see Death as the empat   nost precious yearnings for life, while the warmongers among us turn out to be the real Grim Reapers of death. Read *The Letter from Death* and you will look at death—and life in a newly liberated way. David Moats' illustrations, sometimes chilling, always provocative, make the imagination glow."

Michael McConnell, *American Friends Service Committee, a Quaker organization for peace and social justice*

"Lillian Moats does a remarkable job of bringing Death to life in *The Letter from Death*. … Oddly enough, I finished this book with a smile and a sense of optimism. I'm confident others will feel the same.

Hemant Mehta, *Author of* I Sold My Soul on eBay, *Chair of the Secular Student Alliance*

D1218271

The Letter from Death

The Letter from Death

Lillian Moats

Illustrations by **David J Moats**

Foreword by **Howard Zinn**

THREE
ARTS
PRESS

Downers Grove
Illinois

Fic
Moats

THREE ARTS PRESS

© 2009 by Three Arts Press
Text © 2007 by Lillian Moats
Artwork © 2008 by David Moats

Published 2009 by Three Arts Press. All rights reserved. This book may not be reproduced in whole or in part without written permission from the publisher, except by a reviewer who may quote brief passages in a review. No part of this book may be reproduced, stored in a retrieval system, or transmitted in any form or by any means electronic, mechanical, photocopied, recorded, or other, without written permission from the publisher.

Publisher's Cataloging-in-Publication
(Provided by Quality Books, Inc.)

Moats, Lillian.
    The letter from Death / Lillian Moats ; illustrated
by David J. Moats ; with a foreword by Howard Zinn. —
1st ed.
    p. cm.
    Includes bibliographical references.
    LCCN 2008911147
    ISBN-13: 978-0-9669576-3-1
    ISBN-10: 0-9669576-3-6

    1. Death (Personification)—Fiction. 2. Political
fiction, American.   I. Title.

PS3569.O6523L48 2009   813'.54
                    QBI08-200012

Prepress by John Lord at Graphics Plus Inc.
Printed in USA on acid free paper by Graphics Plus Inc.
3 5 7 9 10 8 6 4 2
First Edition

To Lilian Hauser Dreiser
and "the magical friendship—
quick and deep."

CONTENTS

FOREWORD

Lillian Moats gives us, in *The Letter from Death*, a brilliant and strikingly original work of the imagination, drawing both on biblical scholarship and contemporary military doctrine, infused with wit and irony, grounded in a profound aversion to war and a celebration of human potential for peace.

She starts with a provocative premise, that our fear of death is an obstacle to our understanding of life, that this fear is used by those in power to seduce us into violence and hatred. Moats uses death not as a threat, but as a prism through which to examine the most profound questions that confront the human race today. Her ruminations on hell, and how it has been used through the ages, are both funny and troubling, a mini-education in how our culture distorts our perceptions.

She quietly skewers the blaming of war on "human nature," and draws on the research of respected military historians to tell us the untold story of the natural aversion of soldiers to killing. She also reminds us of what we easily forget: the universal longing of infants for warmth and affection, surely a more powerful resource to draw on than the superficial layers of a culture that denies our deepest needs.

What more authoritative voice can we listen to, in rejecting the violence of war, than that of Death itself? This brief meditation has beauty and eloquence on every page, and it is accompanied by a set of wonderful illustrations by David Moats, the author's son.

Howard Zinn,
Historian, activist, playwright, and author of
A People's History of the United States *and*
You Can't be Neutral on a Moving Train

To Those It May Concern,

That should leave none of you out. Or should I say, "To Those *I* May Concern"? A puny word—"concern"—for your terror of me. You can't imagine the ironies I find in your hatred of me—your hatred of me as the "enemy of life" (which may be the only idea you have ever united around). Am I the enemy of life? No. I am passive. You are the enemies of life! How many of your own kind have you killed over these millennia? Murder, neglect—your beloved wars. And you call *me* the "Grim Reaper." What do you know of me? Nothing!

§

"Grim Reaper"—hardly the worst persona you have fashioned for me. Do I need to assure you I have no scythe to cut off your life? At least in Voodoo, I'm accorded a little humor, allowed dark glasses and a top hat.

Over the ages, you've made vile gods, goddesses, angels and lords of me. Other animals don't dread me. But by the time you began burying your dead, crude conjecture pricked your brains. I can deconstruct your bewilderment. When the deceased had been gored by a predator or bludgeoned by your enemy, the cause of death was evident. Maybe you witnessed the violence yourself. But when a fellow just slumped and died beside you, what to make of it? The corpse was "proof" of an attack—the attacker more fearsome for being invisible.

Unimpeded by skepticism, you created for me one heinous persona after another. In Summeria, you named me *Ereshkigal,* Queen of Death, imagined me a naked demon. Elegant robes you gave my sister, Queen Inanna. All of Heaven and Earth, in fact, you deemed her share of creation. My share? "The Land of No Return," a huge communal grave where spirits moaned and ate dust in eternal darkness. I've been liberally afforded such generosity as this.

In Egypt, you named me *Anubis*, god of the dead, fitted me with a jackal head. When demoted to judge of the dead—vis-à-vis the rise of lord of the dead, Osiris—Anubis received a consolation prize: little golden scales, so practical for weighing your newly dead hearts. Any heart outweighing an ostrich feather would be devoured in the crocodile jaws of my hippopotamus-hindquartered, lion-clawed sidekick Ammit.

Names and versions of Lord *Yama* in Asia varied by region and by systems of belief ... Vedic, Hindu, Buddhist. *Yama*, *Yen-lo*, *Emma-o* meant "god of death" or "king of hell" or one of many kings of many hells. You imagined for Yama a mace with which to club you and a noose

Over the ages, you've made vile
gods, goddesses, angels and lords of me.

to drag you to my underworld for judgment as I rode astride my fierce black buffalo. "Majestic" you sometimes called me—interesting descriptor for one with green skin, sharp fangs, blood red robes and eyes. Diplomatic, though, considering your fate if you displeased me, described in the Tibetan Book of the Dead, the *Barbo Thodol:*

> Yama, The Lord of Death, will place round thy neck a rope and drag thee along; he will cut off thy head, extract thy heart, pull out thy intestines, lick up thy brains, drink thy blood, eat thy flesh, and gnaw thy bones; but thou wilt be incapable of dying. Although the body be hacked to pieces, it will revive again.

Your fantasy—not mine!

I received a slight reprieve in Greece as *Thanatos*, twin brother of Sleep. Over time, I became more beautiful, less threatening ... apparently boring to you as well. How else can you explain the preferential attention paid in Greek myth and literature to *Hades*, king of the underworld and master of Cerberus, a snarling, three-headed dog?

Among the Maya, the god of death and earthquakes was called *Cizan*. In other words, you named me "Stinking One." As your malevolent underworld deity, I had no lack of incarnations—*Ah Puch, Xibalba, Yum Cimil.* As Ah Puch, god of death with an owl's head, I ruled the ninth and cruelest hell of all, *Mitnal.* Aztecs renamed it *Mictlan*, whereupon I, too, underwent a change. As *Mictlantecuhtli*, you took away my owl's head, left me only a headdress of feathers. Nothing to wear on my blood-stained skeleton except a "death collar," a charming necklace of human eyeballs dangling from nerve cords, which I inherited from my former persona Cizan. How you loved that get-up! In a temple at the "navel of the world" you sacrificed chosen impersonators of me. For the record, I've never appreciated being used as your excuse for brutal killing.

Both my Germanic name and that of my underworld were *Hel*, later appropriated as *Hell*, which you have so broadly applied in English. Was it Christian influence over Norse belief that caused the drastic shift in Hel's persona? Let your scholars argue. I was once a sad but gracious goddess welcoming dead souls to my palace. I became a rotting corpse instead, devouring human brains and marrow. Whatever influence revised me, you believed in my makeover. You even witnessed me on my three-legged horse as I gathered victims of plague or famine for my frozen underworld. Only those of you who died in battle could avoid Hel. The import of this last statement probably escaped you just now. Oh, your beloved wars! Not the innocents who perished by plague or famine, but only those who died *while killing* were spared Hel.

What better captured your lust for death in battle than your narratives of me as *Morrigan*, Celtic shape-changing goddess: "goddess of war," "queen of the ghosts," "goddess of the underworld"? You tried to pass off your perversity as mine,

Why have you tormented yourselves—
why have you insulted me—
with such fantasies?

pretending *I* savored setting men at war, joined battles myself, raged about the battlefield like a fury. My frequent form was a carrion crow hovering above the dead. But you might also spy me disguised as the "Washer at the Ford," who chose the next to die in battle. How did I let you know whose death was imminent? You could see me, *ahead of time*, scrubbing his bloody clothes.

In the Hebrew Bible, I appeared as the Angel of Death, *Samael*—"the venom of God." How appropriate, since you thought I killed your kind by thrusting my sword (on whose tip is a drop of gall) into your open mouths. According to the Talmud, Satan and I are one. This allows you to see me as the epitome of evil: seducer, accuser, destroyer. As Samael, I commanded legions of demons, navigated the skies on my twelve wings. I was the serpent who tempted the first pair of you in the Garden of Eden. You credit me, Samael, for spoiling your unblemished world.

As the Angel of Death I went unnamed in the Qur'an. But in the Islamic literature that followed,

did you not outdo yourselves? I was called *'Izra'il*.
Cosmic in size, I stood with one foot on the
knife-sharp bridge dividing hell from paradise, the
other foot planted in either the fourth or seventh
heaven. Whether my wings were "numberless" or
totaled precisely 4,000 depended on who was
counting. As for the myriad eyes and tongues
which comprised my body, the sum also kept
changing since it matched the number of you living on the earth.

Why have you tormented yourselves—why have
you insulted me—with such fantasies?   Even
those who laugh them off, laugh nervously. Who
are the monsters? Not me. What your forebears
imagined for themselves still works under the surface of your consciousness.

What do you—what did they—know of me?
Nothing!

§

III

So much for what I am not. Now I'll attempt the harder work—to define myself for the first time. Given the endless ways humanity has maligned me, why do I even bother? I'll get to that later.

In the scheme of things, we all have a part to play. It falls to me to absorb your last breath. I don't determine which breath it will be. In fact, my role is anything but aggressive. But when your life can no longer sustain itself, I have one moment with you, one moment in which to take in your final exhalation.

You can't imagine all that I assimilate in that instant—the sentient remains of a life, the sum of remembrance. If there is suffering near the end, I am your release from that suffering. Contrary to entrenched belief, you have nothing to fear from me.

Nevertheless, how unsettling it may be for you to read this letter. I don't delude myself;

So much for what I am not.

few of you will even pick it up for fear of being seen as "morbidly inclined." If you've read this far, at least you've shown a trace of independence. I have many things to say to you. If you can tolerate the provocation, you're unlikely to see me the same way again.

As much as you'd like to deny it, there has never been life without me. I've existed on this earth for millions of years. I can't claim to remember my early relationship with plants and the simplest animals. I could not have had a real relationship with them, or even with myself at the time. As a mere functionary, I cared nothing for any of you. But as life evolved into greater and greater complexity I, too, changed incrementally. You know only intellectually what I know by direct experience: it has taken eons for consciousness to evolve.

Since my perceptions are derived from those I've taken in from you and other complex creatures, you might conclude that my awareness has grown in parallel with yours. But that would not account for the stark difference in my perspective. And the difference *is* stark. It's my simultaneous presence—here, there—wherever life is ending, as well as the long span of my conscious memory, that causes me to focus on your patterns, endlessly repeated patterns. Endlessly repeated folly. I'll tell you outright that over the millennia, my feelings toward humanity have polarized.

In all of those singular moments I have with you as individuals, how could I be unresponsive to you? Over the ages, I've absorbed so much of your sorrow, I'm imbued with it. I am more vast with your sorrows than your joys, since the ends of your lives are so often colored by the consciousness of parting. I meet you most often when you've lost your bluff and swagger, when you're stripped down to vulnerability. In your solitude, I seldom find you hard to comprehend.

Yet, having assimilated human sensitivities, how can I regard your collective insensitivities with anything but disgust? Your societies profess to love "Truth" even as you subvert it. I'm stultified by your concerted capacity for self-deception, and your devotion to the myths with which you rationalize your communal actions and inaction. It is the resulting destructiveness of your species that I find abhorrent.

No matter how you behave, I'll simply continue the work that falls to me. But I can't resist asking you questions that torment me. I'll be blunt: is your species incapable of even the most rudimentary observation?

§

What evidence suggests that I will
be a gateway to justice?

IV

Look around you. Do you see a universe in-fused with fairness? Does the earthquake select its victims with discerning care, the hurricane spare the most innocent or vulnerable?

I want to make a point here—about the amorality of the universe, knowing that most of you will still protest *Everything is part of God's in-tricate plan*. From my perspective on your history, which extends its full length, it has not been long since most of you would have said *Everything is up to the whims of the gods*. Now most of you con-sider it more advanced to worship one God. But which explanation—the capriciousness of gods or the wisdom of one God—captures the utter sense-lessness when a man's meager parcel of land slides down the mountain? When a poet, in her prime, full of faith, dies of leukemia? When a desiccated breast is all that a mother has to offer her starving baby?

Look around you. What evidence suggests that

I will be a gateway to justice, that you will die and thereby find every inequity set right?

How you crave justice. Yet, how you fear it. Or should I say, how you fear punishment and crave reward? When you think of me—when you think past me to concoct an afterlife—what wishful thinking, fear and guilt stoke your imaginations!

Yet, not in equal proportions. Heaven may be variously described in your holy books: celestial gardens, jeweled trees, rivers of milk and honey, delightful paths to be wandered in your resplendent bodies—some of those bodies winged. (An absence of sweat and stench has been specifically noted.) But historically, your religious leaders have been most apt to say of Heaven: *"What God has prepared for us, cannot be imagined by the human mind."* This can hardly be said of Hell!

§

V

Your fear of me has been almost indistinguishable from your fear of what comes after me. You have had anxious questions. Masses of you have been taken in by those who claim to have authoritative answers. Hardly is there a religion on earth that has not devised a Hell with which to manipulate your guilt. Whenever death is linked with punishment, my reputation is unjustly smeared. Therefore I'll take the trouble to expose some of the absurdity.

Hell has become, of course, an embarrassment to a great many of you. It is only a metaphor, you insist, for what you call the "dark night of the soul." I think there's more to Hell than that—not as actuality, but in your psychology. As long as many of you believe that hellish punishment will be everlasting, and others that it will be transitory between incarnations, Hell's importance to the human psyche can hardly be dismissed.

If you think I am not speaking to you—if you

think you are free of such superstitions—think again. For thousands of years, Hell has fed your species' guilty imaginations, your masochism, sadism, black humor and dread. At the very least it lives on in each of you as an unconscious legacy. The minds of those who have come before you were permeated with Hell-fears. Sacred passages have been so often pressed upon you in your final hours, that I can easily parrot them back to you.

Your nervous questions about Hell have been human questions, virtually the same among peoples and religions. I will draw on the phantasmagoria of the Christian Hell for answers—though the threat of punishment has hardly been confined to that Faith.

Who goes to Hell?

Considering the high stakes, one might have expected the official response to have been "violent criminals." Instead, sex achieved preeminent focus on a growing list of damnable offenses, especially after Saint Augustine tied it firmly to

"original sin."   Then, of course, there are the
deadly sins: pride, envy, anger, avarice, sloth, glut-
tony, lust. Did you know sadness was one of the
seven until it was bumped by sloth?

Such disconcerting teachings fade next to the
Elucidarium, which, for centuries, spelled out
church doctrine to aid uneducated priests. In
brief, they were instructed to tell you that God has
always known who would go to Hell and who to
Heaven, and that most of you would be tortured
eternally—an arrangement designed by the
Almighty for the gratification of the Elect.
Berthold of Regensburg, preacher of renown, came
up with the numbers: only one in 100,000 of you
would be saved. Given that calculation, you might
find consolation in the reported testimony of a deceased hermit. Among the 30,000 who died the
same day as St. Bernard, only one other soul en-
tered Heaven. (The other being none other than
the hermit.) Apparently on a good day one in
15,000 could be saved—a considerably more opti-
mistic bit of data.

Do people really burn in Hell?

Absolutely, was the answer. But the unexpected—not to say "protracted"—delay of the Second Coming and Last Judgment did create a conundrum. Since bodies of the deceased will not be resurrected until that time, the idea of an extended reprieve from physical torment might embolden sinners. What line of reasoning could keep them in tow? Saint Augustine puzzled it out. The soul's capacity for physical suffering is virtually identical before and after the body's resurrection because the soul carries inside it a sort of mental model of the body it inhabited—complete with sensory perceptions. The first judgment on the soul takes place immediately after death, the Saint declared. Why then, after enduring untold ages of thoroughly convincing burning, it would be necessary for a soul to reenter the body to receive its just desserts remains a mystery to me.

Whether the resurrected bodies of the damned would be spiritual or "solid" was, according to Augustine, unworthy of deliberation—as long as the damned bodies fulfilled two absolute requirements: They must be capable of feeling pain, while incapable of dying.

In case fiery admonitions were still lost on you, saintly reinforcement mounted. Some had a gift for visualization. Saint Brigit of Sweden (reported by her maid to be of benign and gentle demeanor—in fact, given to laughter) could see fire boiling up through the feet of embodied souls, blazing through their veins, and blasting through their brains, their ears acting like bellows.

Eight centuries after Augustine, Thomas Aquinas reaffirmed the physicality of Hellfire, as well as the pleasure to be derived from watching others burn.

How long does the suffering last?

Clergy reported to their illiterate flocks that the Bible's prescription for sinners was everlasting punishment. For those of you who found "everlasting" too abstract, Berthold of Regensburg, again, was helpful: imagine your torments lasting for as many thousand years as the drops

*Hardly is there a religion on earth
that has not devised a Hell with which
to manipulate your guilt.*

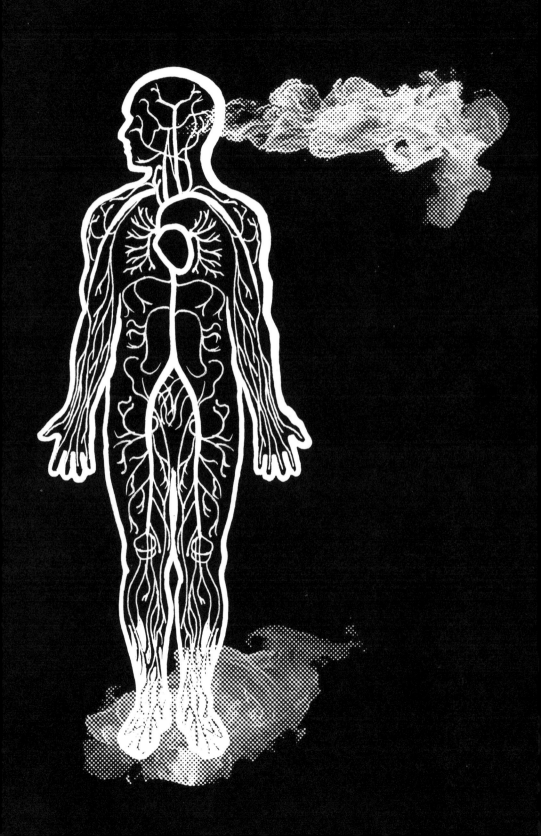

that comprise the ocean—or as the number of hairs that have grown on humankind and beasts since the act of creation. Now have you got it? Not really. At that point, according to Berthold, your pains will have just begun.

Is there any hope of avoiding Hell?

As with so many aspects of life, the answer came back, "For the right price." Before the Reformation, you could purchase "indulgences" for the remission of punishment, if you had the means. Better still, you could employ someone less fortunate to make a pilgrimage or simply to pray, or fast or flagellate himself on your behalf.

The Reformation offered no reprieve from Hell fear; it was back to basics. Catholic inventions such as Purgatory and the Virgin Intercessor were discarded. For everlasting punishment, Luther's Hell matched Augustine's. According to many of the Reformers, you are either a member of the "saved" or a member of the "reprobates." Given that deadly sins are committed by both, only God's mysterious mercy allows the first group to be

spared. This is no small demonstration of His le-
niency if you bear in mind Calvin's assessment of
humanity: "nothing but mud and filth" within and
without.

*Are there other things to fear in Hell besides
fire?*

Christians have been warned that Hell is not
only where "the fire is not quenched," but where
"the worm never sleepeth." Dashing any hope
that the worm might be singular, the *Apocalypse of
Peter* informed you there is such a population of
them in one underworld location that they amass
into a dark cloud.

If you were obsessed with control, the author
of *Peter* reassured you that rebellious slaves and
children could look forward to torture. But then,
so might you. If after, say, eons, one of the
damned should forget the nature of his earthly of-
fense, Peter's schema would ensure that the apt-
ness of punishments jogged the sinner's memory.
"Why am I hanging over this pit of smoldering
sewage—by my tongue? Oh, now I remember,"

the blasphemer might muse. Perpetrators of sins of the flesh needn't wonder why they are repeatedly flayed.

More torments were added in the *Apocalypse of Paul*, along with snow and an icy pit on the west side of Hell. Also detailed was an elaborate surveillance system. At birth you are assigned a guardian angel who rarely leaves your side except for twice-daily debriefings to God (noon and midnight) regarding your every deed. In spite of their efforts at positive influence, some angels end up with intransigent sinners. Be warned: an angel spurned might have an axe to grind after you die! In the underworld, they can become avenging angels with jutting teeth, sparks flying from their mouths and hair. As such, they wield an impressive array of instruments of torture—razors and chains for instance, both red-hot.

Through the centuries, Hell's torments accrued until the Counter-Reformation. The Jesuits observed that the more wealthy and sophisticated of their flock had become jaded by the usual

Be warned: an angel spurned might have
an axe to grind after you die!

histrionics. Hell was revamped to reclaim this desirable audience. Tortures were eliminated; the obligatory worms and fire specified in the Bible were maintained. To elicit maximum revulsion from the powerfully rich, a slum-like, over-populated, reeking cesspool of a Hell was contrived wherein the damned—bloated, infected—were crammed belly to bum. The unconvinced were advised to think of weeping sores, feces and putrid breath. It was one thing to burn in Hell, another to burn with the "lower classes."

Where is Hell located?

For hundreds of years, Hell's exact whereabouts were debated, though generally presumed to be beneath the flat earth, Heaven being above. It was self-evident to those who heard cries and groans from within Vesuvius that volcanoes were Hell's entrances.

Once the earth achieved a roundness in your minds, Hell relocated to earth's center. No enduring threat to theology: Heaven was still up, Hell was down. But in 1714 science began to challenge even those ground rules. The Royal Society's Tobias Swinden published *An Enquiry into the Nature and Place of Hell*. Previously, the German theologian Drexelius had estimated the damned-to-date to be a hundred thousand million, compacted into a subterranean cavity one German mile square. Swinden denounced both figures as outrageously paltry. An underground Hell would have insufficient oxygen to fuel the fires, much less adequate dimensions for the burgeoning throngs of reprobates. He proved the sun to be Hell's site.

Swinden's theory accounted for the fires of Hell, but what about the cold? Only a few years later, William Whiston (astronomer, and Cambridge mathematics professor appointed by Isaac Newton) posited Hell's location to be a comet. Its path would take it close to the sun's heat, as well as the cold near Saturn.

Has any mortal been there and returned?

Eye-witness accounts were provided. Most of Hell's tourists had a supernatural guide; others simply died and lived to tell about it. (I wasn't informed of these "deaths.") With stories recorded by literate clergy, often based on accounts by common folk, "vision literature" proliferated for a thousand years.

The first narrative, written down by Pope Saint Gregory the Great, told of a monk who, having died, visited countless places in Hell where he witnessed famous people hanging in flames. Like many a vision survivor, he was revived by his guide—with an admonition to improve his behavior.

More than 600 years passed before the genre reached the level of *The Vision of Tundale* in 1149. This treasure, written by an Irish Monk, was translated into no less than twelve languages. It seems that, prompted by a stroke, the soul of the charming, lustful knight Tundale left his body for a couple of horrific days in Hell. He was greeted by a sarcastic throng of fiends demanding: Where are all the pretty maids now? Why are you not fornicating? His guardian angel arranged an instructive tour, assisting him across a thousand foot long

Has any mortal been there
and returned?

plank which spanned a stinking valley. Inconveniently for Tundale, his angel vanished just when he stood before the awful beast Acheron, taller than any mountain Tundale had ever seen. Opportunistic fiends instantly heaved the unprotected knight into the belly of the beast, wherein he was treated to a Hell sampler: burned, frozen, overcome by sulphur, bitten by serpents, bears, lions and rabid dogs, bludgeoned by devils—all before a temporary rescue.

Tundale found that the particulars of the first narrow bridge were trumped by a second, which spanned a turbulent lake, brimming with hungry beasts. Two miles in length, not quite as wide as a human hand, the bridge was abundantly pierced with nails which made it something of a dilemma whether to continue shredding one's feet or throw oneself into the ravenous mouths below. Tundale's angel declined to accompany him, but the knight would not be crossing alone. His assignment was to lead a wild cow, in punishment for the one he had stolen from his neighbor. Every inch of progress was hard-won. Then, mid-bridge, a dramatic stand-off ensued during which an approaching soul begged Tundale not to take up the entire width. Apparently, even the narrator of Tundale's story couldn't figure out how to get them out of their predicament, for he reported lamely that neither Tundale nor the other soul knew how it happened that they passed by each other.

Tundale's trials were far from over, however. Among them, he was subjected to the same punishment as libidinous priests and nuns. They were impregnated and eaten by a huge, winged beast with an iron beak. Vomited into a frozen swamp, they endured the difficult gestation of their fetuses. Like vipers, the developing young stirred and stung the innards of the holy sinners until they (priests and nuns alike) gave excruciating birth from every limb and orifice to spiked-tailed, iron-beaked serpents. Vision literature titillated as much as it terrified.

The enormous success of Hellfire sermons inspired local clergy to initiate Mystery Plays in

which they, themselves, performed to educate
their illiterate congregations. Eventually the art
form provided the common man creative license of
his own. For six centuries more or less, beginning
with the tenth, the plays grew in scale and inno-
vation (until the church again tightened its grip).
Most mystery cycles began with Adam and Eve and
ended with the Second Coming. Animal entrails
assisted in the art of moral persuasion, along with
wooden heads and trick limbs. Two hundred and
twenty actors delivered thirty-five thousand
verses in the Paris cycle. Yearly in York, your
bleary-eyed forebears gathered at four-thirty in
the morning to witness forty-eight different dra-
mas on a single day.

How could the rambunctious staging of Hell
not have become the ultimate crowd pleaser with
oversized puppet monsters, smoke-belching props,
flames shot from trapdoors and sulfurous explo-
sions? Townships competed, and in the cities,
each tradesmen's guild was assigned a portion of
these Biblical extravaganzas. Hell scenes became

the pride of the cooks and bakers. Who could be more adept with smoke and fire? Who better supplied with cauldrons, spits and other implements of torture? What better sound effects for the din of Hell than the cacophony of pots and pans?

The tradesmen's valiant attempts to fight horror with humor eventually devolved, causing inordinate attention to be devoted to the subject of passing gas. By the later Middle Ages, if you, yourself, had won the role of Lucifer, you might have been rewarded with the challenge of breathing fire while gripping two firecrackers—not to mention the one specified for your rump.

Shall I draw the curtain here on Hell's preposterousness?

§

VI

Your fear and guilt have been exploited for centuries because of the mystery surrounding me. For my sake as well as yours, I would have liked nothing better than to explode the myths. But with no words to utter, I could do nothing but appreciate your trustworthy doubts, which enabled you—if only for fleeting moments of relief—to laugh. This voice of mine, which still feels alien to me, must have been rising in me imperceptibly for ages, though it seems to have broken out abruptly. I did not know that accumulated frustration and anger could one day cause me to find a voice.

I will have to make do using this device of yours—this tool of language in which your species takes so much pride. But how inadequate words feel to me. I don't know how you endure the perpetual search for the right one, when at best the right word only circumscribes whatever it tries to represent: like a cage, it captures the bird, but ends its flight.

Silence is my medium. Nothing is lost in trans-lation. In silence I assimilate the mingled emo-tions that no word has ever touched. Even metaphor—the most artful tool you've invented—is for me a concession. In the very act of describ-ing myself, have I constructed a cage from which I'll long to escape?

§

VII

I've addressed imaginary hells with you. Now I
can delay no longer the task I've assigned myself:
to confront you with the hell of your own making—the palpable one, lacking in humor, but not
lacking in horror.

Who goes to this hell?

Any one of you might, especially if you're pow-
erless. It has nothing to do with moral worth.
Simply being seen as "the other" can make you a
candidate.

How long does the suffering last?

The anguish of some seems to them everlasting. Some are instantly eradicated.

Are there things to fear in this hell besides fire?

Consider bullets, shrapnel, land mines ... the
possibility of torture; disfigurement; loss of limbs,
eyes, senses and sanity; the suffering or annihila-
tion of everyone you love.

Where is such a hell located?

It is transient. You could go to this hell; it

could come to you.

Has any mortal been there and returned?

Millions have returned, though not necessarily whole. In any case, they are never the same.

Is there any hope of avoiding this hell?

For the individual, it remains largely a matter of fortune. As for your species—I am no more clairvoyant than you.

The torments you feared from your gods, you've devised for your enemies, and have realized for yourselves.

§

VIII

Millions have burned in this hell of yours.
Last century, the numbers grew exponentially.
One might conclude your fear of one another is
inexhaustible, but underlying your militarism is
your fear of *me*. Your dictum appears to be:
Using any means necessary, force your enemies
to face death before they can force you to do
the same. It does not appear to matter whether
the threat you feel from them is real or imagined. In war after war, you have chosen to send
wave after wave of your barely grown children to
meet me, rather than face me yourselves.

Are you incapable of seeing patterns? Are
you hampered by the narrow scope of individual
memory?

A stick or stone can be enough to kill an
enemy. But your enemy, too, might pick up a
stick or stone. Carving a well-weighted club,
though, gave you a fleeting sense of invulnera-
bility, until an enemy made a well-weighted

The torments you feared from your gods,
you've devised for your enemies, and
have realized for yourselves.

club. Then you needed to lash a rock to the end
of your club before you felt the thrill you
needed to counteract your fear.

Tell me, what weapon finally proved to make
you invincible? Was it the spear? "No," I hear
you say, your enemy also made a spear. The
sword, then? Or the double-edged sword? The
bow and arrow? The composite bow? The war
chariot? No—not even armadas of war chariots!
The warship with battering ram? The torsion artillery of the ballista that allowed you to shoot
heavy stones? No? Then certainly when it was
superseded by the catapult with which you
could launch boulders five hundred yards. Still
no? "Greek fire" then! The catapult could also
launch Greek fire, a mixture of chemicals that
would explode into flames. Impressive. But you
say not even Greek fire actually made you invincible?

Let's skip ahead to the longbow. Its aerody-
namic arrow could penetrate your enemy's armor,
his vital organs, his horse's saddle and kill his

horse. Surely becoming accomplished longbow-men made at least some of you invincible. No? Then the crossbow?

How about gun powder? Cannon? Then, better steel and better shells? The submarine? The machine gun?—itself responsible for more deaths than any other weapon. What about a machine gun mounted on a tank? No?

You could wipe out entire armies when you filled the warheads of artillery shells with poison gases. Yet you were still not invincible, you say?

How about distancing from your enemies? Perhaps this gave you what you were looking for—a more god-like view. Bombing people from the sky must have finally, finally done it for you. No? The *atomic* bomb, then. Surely, to inflict a Pandora's box of horror from the skies— vaporize your enemy, melt his eyes and flesh, poison him over his lifetime—must have finally made you invincible. No? The hydrogen bomb, then. To terrorize and bully one another, you stockpiled tens of thousands of nuclear war-heads. Congratulations! You could end life as you know it.

While nuclear warfare was put on precarious hold, you relied on weapons you did not hesitate to use. Napalm, for instance. Fire-bombing, too, was excellent at sucking oxygen from the lungs of burning victims—without that unfortunate stigma of all things nuclear.

Did laser- and satellite-guided missiles satisfy? On the contrary. Ironically, many construe their relative precision to be a rationale for a new generation of missiles armed with nuclear bombs that will be "perfectly suited" for the battlefield.

Meanwhile, don't you think if you could attack and fend off enemies from *space* you would be invincible? Why don't you work on it? I see. You already are. While you're at it, biological warfare is awfully crude. Perhaps you should see how science could weaponize, say, genetic

Tell me what weapon finally
made you invincible?

engineering, nanotechnology. Why not draw up plans for robotic warfare?

You are, of course. Across your world, on your behalf, more than half a million of your most brilliant scientists are working on such "advancements" of war.

Yet, you call *me* the "Grim Reaper!"

§

IX

What on earth have you been thinking of? Are you not inherently vulnerable? Did you have to invent unnatural horrors? Droughts were not enough for you? Nor floods, nor hurricanes? Famine was not enough? Infestations, pandemics? Were the inescapable diminishments of aging not enough to make you face the frailty you all share?

No. Because the fact that you will one day *cease to exist* is what you have turned your world upside-down to avoid. Intellectually, you may accept my inevitability, but emotionally, what I find in you is an inexhaustible genius for denial.

I have said your fear of me drives your militarism. I have also said you deny to yourselves that you will ever die. A contradiction? I am only mirroring your mental contortions.

Do I think I am the *only* reason for your militarism? I am not that myopic. I insist, though, that both your fear of me and your denial of that fear are hidden reasons for your killing. And whatever you hide from yourselves takes on inordinate power. I take no joy in pointing out your illusions—but I refuse to pander to them.

I could say, as you sometimes do, "Don't shoot the messenger!" But then, what would that mean, given who I am?

§

What on earth have you been thinking of?
Are you not inherently vulnerable?

X

To state my frank opinion, neither religion nor science nor technology (nor any other -ism or -ology) will save you. Yet, why would I bother to address you if I did not think you had the potential to save yourselves? I would simply pity the whole lot of you if I believed humanity to be condemned by its genetic make-up—or some "fall from grace"—to endlessly repeat atrocities.

Doubtless, you have concluded from my railing against the widespread violence of your species that I think human beings are *naturally* prone to killing their own kind. How little you know me still. I don't think anything of the sort.

Throughout your long history, I have experienced every one of your societies. Their distinctive relations to warfare I have learned through the psyches of their peoples. I have assimilated cultures that engaged in no warring; some that, to obviate the need for killing, created ceremonial outlets for conflict. I have known ritualistic warfare, in which the killing of a single member of an enemy group constituted a victory respected by both sides. I have absorbed both ancient and current cultures that have institutionalized the neurosis of retaliation, cultures that slaughter and torture—need I say "pathologically?"

In reporting that some form of war has been built into myriad cultures, I do not endorse the claim that concerted violence is bound to find expression in you. It is the collective credulity with which you accept and pass along a culture's approval of war that astounds and alarms me.

You excuse human behavior by pointing to that of primates from which you evolved. You shrug, "Violence is just part of our animal nature." But you are as closely related to the gentle, matriarchal bonobo ape as to the aggressive chimpanzee. Tell me, why have so few of you even heard of them? And why are you rarely taught about those human societies that have so valued peace that they have devised effective measures to foster it?

My role demands I come to all living things

privately—requiring a concurrently distant and close-up point of view. Could there be anything more wrenching than the contrast I find between what you now call the "macro" and "micro?" Why do individuals behave so differently in groups? No one could speak with more intimate knowledge than I about the instinctive aversion you have *as individuals* to killing your own kind, and the toll such a primal act can exact from the killer.

I don't have in mind the sociopaths among you, or the endless parade of politicians who manipulate and conscript adolescents to kill and die for them. At this moment, I'm thinking of countless soldiers whose private agonies have been so ignored in the war myths you call "history."

The natural resistance to killing another of your species is reinforced in childhood by every moral teaching. Then, with each nation's support, its military shames and trains its youth to kill. Do you think a conscience can be permanently suppressed?

Since your earliest warring—and more

*You are as closely related to
the gentle, matriarchal bonobo ape
as to the aggressive chimpanzee.*

commonly than you might guess—I've taken in dying gasps of young boys who made easy targets of themselves, immobilized with horror after their first kill. In your most destructive century, I absorbed the final breaths of decorated World War veterans still haunted by the photographs of infants they found on the corpses of the "enemy." Far outnumbering these are my memories of soldiers who desperately disguised an inability to kill, even as they died saving their comrades. I know that the war stories you are used to hearing are not like these. Such accounts of personal anguish are censored or drowned out by the more "heroic" kind.

Why are histories of warfare written? Justification by the victors is a covert motive I discern. "Never forget the triumphs and sacrifices of our side," your leaders implore you. But by what maniacal reckoning must more and ever more youths die so none will have "died in vain"?

While you have been repeating by rote the presumption of war as necessary evil, powerful militaries across your world have applied themselves to the widespread "problem" of young men reluctant to kill. Not to worry! Desensitizing solutions have already been found: slick propaganda, relentless practice in virtual killing, overexposure to glorified brutality. Are you relieved to know that, for soldiers conditioned by such techniques, the firing rate has more than quadrupled since your Second World War?

My outrage at the growing militarism of your species does not blind me to the more subtle and varied traits I find in individuals. I admire that human quality—call it compassion, empathy?— that still makes it nearly impossible for most of you to kill. Do you find this ironic—Death admiring those who cannot kill? Then how little you know me, even yet.

§

78

XI

You call death—you call *me*—"The Great Leveler." This, I detest. Why would I want to be used this way, as paltry consolation to those who have been made or kept poor; or worse, as rationalization for the greedy to plunder while they can? The Great Leveler!—as if, when I meet your kind, it is not entirely too late to correct the inequities you have wrought.

None of you enters this world more worthy than anyone else. Yet between entering and leaving, every sort of advantage is gained by some people over others. The man whose foot was blown off by a landmine, the woman relegated to child-bearer and water-bearer, the family who sleeps on the sidewalk, the child who scavenges landfills for food, must somehow hold their own against the world's affluent, thriving, educated, liberated. What's more, the children of those who come out ahead are rewarded with multiplied advantages.

By what maniacal reckoning
must more and ever more youths die
so none will have "died in vain?"

Surely you recall from your school days that it was the children most assured of winning who clamored to compete. For longer than any of you can remember, I have witnessed your species follow infantile leaders who, behind their idealistic rhetoric, have set rich against poor, fortunate against hapless while using the complacent among you as leverage.

If truthfully articulated, the program of the winners would read: *"We, the entitled, proclaim our right to control the resources needed by every one of you to survive. We will coerce the poorest among you to exploit nature for our gain. We will deny them a rightful share. We will lead the world in fouling its air and water. The surface of the earth we will litter with explosive devices. We will compound our wealth by selling killing machines to 'friends' and 'enemies' alike."* I would like to think that if you saw such inequity clearly, you would stand up en masse against it. But would *enough* of you?

How ironic that, due in great part to your

collective tolerance for the brinksmanship of the powerful, your survival now utterly depends on justice—fair and careful sharing of dwindling resources. I say again: I am no gateway to justice. If you want justice, you will have to do more than to wait for me and wring your hands.

The complacent among you have excelled, to date, at looking the other way, while the conscientious have pleaded for care of the earth. Even the latter can be blinded by anthropocentrism for— with or without you—the earth itself will adapt and endure, though myriad species including your own are at risk. As the irreplaceable vanishes, do you think there is no tomorrow? Or do you still convince yourself that endless tomorrows await you in some next world? In the spreading wars over resources, I see no inevitable Armageddon— just another unnecessary Hell advancing on earth.

§

XII

I wonder ... do you not know what I know about the inner lives of human beings? How could that be, since I've acquired all of my knowledge from you? The difference must be that I've taken in the emotional legacies of all those who've come before you; whereas each of you is confined to your own skin, never able to live in another's mind—even momentarily as I do. It must be your isolation that makes you susceptible to distortions about humanity at large—such as the conclusion that violent aggression is hopelessly hard-wired into human nature.

But for all my shock at some of the ways you behave in concert, I'll reaffirm that, singly, you are far easier for me to comprehend. I take from each final breath a thousand, thousand distillations—tinctures from childhood and even infancy, traces of your original longing which does not cease until that moment in which I take it in.

*The earth itself will adapt
and endure.*

It would be impossible for you to imagine what I experience at the moment of your death—nearly impossible for me to describe it. I can only employ words I have learned from you. If there were a lexicon to describe my side of the experience, it would need to be even more subtle, nuanced than words you use to distinguish color, flavor, music.

When the actual moment occurs, it is far simpler from your side than mine. My work is something like listening, though of course it is not sound you release to me. I draw in your conscious and unconscious history, the imaginative worlds within you, the ideas that drove you. I "remember" your personal narrative: pivotal encounters, fears, euphoria, your dreams and the turns of your disillusionment. All of this occurs with a simultaneity unimaginable for you who are so bound by time.

I could not translate into words the unspoken motivations I absorb from any human being who has lived more than a few years. You all have

My work is something like listening.

needs—bodily and emotional. They become more urgent if they go unmet. Your efforts to satisfy them may become, by your life's end, so twisted and out of scale that I must trace them back to your earliest hours in order to understand you. But I never interpret complexity as randomness. There are reasons for your actions, no matter how layered.

How could I think of human beings in your simplistic terms "good" or "evil" when I have overwhelming evidence that *conditions* can exact, from any one of you, extreme cruelty or extreme compassion?

I cannot claim that my intimate knowledge of individuals has led me to unerring comprehension of you. On my part, incredulity is a frequent state of mind. Why is it that you do not work harder to create conditions that nurture the qualities you most admire?

The potential for empathy is built into your brains and bodies. A nursing mother's milk flows spontaneously if she feels suddenly and deeply for *any* other being. When I consider the superiority of your heartfelt personal intentions over your often barbaric communal actions, I can't fathom why you rarely think for yourselves, why you rarely speak your minds before authority, why you repeatedly line up behind ideologies, religions and paradigms. Are you so afraid of being alone?

Yet I ask myself how you can think for yourselves if you're not allowed to feel for yourselves? One can't occur without the other.

How rarely are children gently helped to distinguish real from imaginary perceptions. Too often, their candid observations are undermined by a stern imposition of arbitrary beliefs. Too often, they are told that they should not feel what is most natural for them to feel. The stifling of your adult ideas and emotions begins with your humiliation in childhood.

A person who must suppress "unacceptable" emotions all his life can be manipulated unwittingly. His forbidden feelings become, at last, no longer identifiable as his own. He imagines them, instead, to be the untrustworthy traits of others. Then how easily he can be persuaded by the rhetoric of powerful leaders to project those traits onto outsiders—that is to say, onto *the other*.

§

XIII

With stunning frequency you go to war against the other, based on a concept of "good versus evil." But when it comes to protecting your boundaries—tribal, national, and personal—I find that you more often mean "evil versus purity." Every organism has a boundary, yet only humans suffer confusion and angst about what is inside versus what is outside. Again and again I witness your fear of contamination.

You have a bodily skin without a corresponding psychological border. You can project yourselves imaginatively forward and back in time, into deep space, onto the ocean's floor, atop the most forbidding mountain, into earth's core. Some can visualize a subatomic world no eye can see. You attempt to explore the innermost motivations of friends and strangers. The edges of your experience cannot be circumscribed.

It is understandably difficult, at times, to distinguish between imagination and action, between inner and outer, mental and physical life. But how much easier it would be to integrate these natural dualities if you did not cling to the concepts of evil and purity implanted in your childhoods. And how much less you would find yourselves guarding your personal boundaries.

It strikes me as bizarre that you see evidence for the existence of evil only in the behavior of your own kind. You do not call violent weather "evil," though whole cities can be ripped apart by storms. You are more likely to call them "acts of God." You do not label predatory animals "evil," though they may eat alive their screaming prey. Only in deceitful or vicious acts committed by fellow humans do you find confirmation that evil is alive and active in the world.

In all that I have taken in from you, I have found no evidence for this *force* you call "evil"— though I hardly need to reiterate my outrage at millions of heinous acts. Why would you persist in believing that a force you confirm only by human actions is supernatural in its might? It must be because this fantastical notion simplifies your collective lives. How much easier it is to blame an inscrutable force than to probe the complex causes of human behavior, or to create conditions least likely to elicit destructive acts.

"Combating evil" provides your leaders with an ever-ready rationale for war. In the word "evil" itself is imbedded a consensus for drastic action; if an evil force exists, your collective will should be compelled to overcome it wherever it manifests itself. When you are persuaded that it is expressed in the actions of another nation, race, ethnicity, you pretend to make war against evil itself, not against their flesh and blood, which you know in your heart of hearts to be the same as yours.

§

XIV

Your species has imagined pure and imperish-
able forms in a transcendent realm. You have
imagined for every individual a final judgment
written indelibly. Yet life on earth consists of con-
tinuous change, progression and entropy. How
could you have devised a more inappropriate
measure for humanity than evil versus purity?

Never mind. I know the history of these no-
tions. It is hardly worth tracing them back to
their roots. So many of you—with or without religion—matter-of-factly incorporate evil, and its
utter absence, into your worldview. How can you
still entertain such absolutes? Whether you attrib-
ute them to religion or philosophy they are no
more than your own psychology to me.

I absorb memories of humiliation from the final
breaths of small children—the same remnants of
early denigration that I take in from the old.
Whether those childhood lessons are stifled from
consciousness or painfully vivid decades later,

How you confuse your children!
How you were confused yourselves.

they color your emotional life through the inter-
vening years.

What is this relentless teaching, conveyed in a
thousand ways? By shaming and approval, you are
taught of the existence of "good" and "bad" emotions. Whether or not the words are ever spoken,
such cumulative visceral lessons comprise every
child's primer on evil and purity.

How you confuse your children! How you were
confused yourselves. Was it that you had to pre-
vent bad feelings from entering you and keep the
good ones in? Or that you had to hide the bad
ones inside you and only let the good ones show?
How can one keep feelings hidden unless one
hides them from oneself?

I would hardly disagree that, as they grow,
children must become answerable for their actions,
but I happen to know most of you were held ac-
countable for much more. You were in good graces
one moment, pushed away the next, if you dis-
played a range of feeling. If a child's emotions
threaten the adults on whom a child utterly de-

pends, how can she, herself, not feel frightened?

How clear it is, from my manifold moments with your kind, that no feeling has been as feared or misunderstood by you as anger. From my vantage point, it is easy to decipher that anger is never more than a secondary emotion, rising up as your protection against a vulnerability. But how few of you are taught as children to look at anger as a pointer to something deeper—frustration, or humiliation, or rejection, jealousy, sadness, grief?

It is no wonder to me that when a child is misunderstood, he will regard his angry feelings as magic—not really *his*, they possess the alien power to tempt him, invade him, contaminate, taint him. How inevitable that he will ultimately deny his own "dangerous" emotions while he casts them outward onto someone else.

Your calamitous fear of feeling hardly ends with childhood. Century after century, I assimilate the final breaths of humans still unconsciously guarding what they deem to be their boundaries. From childhood on, they have been compelled to maintain an illusory purity within, compelled to keep all that is evil out.

To "cleanse" themselves of the evil influence of the other, ethnicities slaughter one another. You fortify and patrol national borders as if they could protect you from what has always been within. Your world contracts as your vigilance expands. Only if you can stop annihilating your fellow human beings might you have time to figure yourselves out.

Meanwhile, if you abandoned the unworthy model of evil versus purity, you might allow yourselves to be tenderly amused—and seriously enlightened—by your children. Any child who is not stifled can make transparent to you the fact that emotions have a logic of their own.

You may go on searching among the living if you choose, but I am frankly relieved that among those of you who have died to date, I have not found one pure human being, much less one who was purely evil.

§

Your world contracts
as your vigilance expands.

XV

In your cynical depictions of me, you imagine I enjoy being the cause of your grief. Do you think I have a choice in the matter?

I am as vast as you've often suspected—not vast in darkness or emptiness, as you've feared— but in the extent of my assimilation of final essences, yours and all the other living things on earth. Your grief has taught me much about the individual human condition—the fragility of your attachments, the pain of bereavement, the immutability of your deepest affections.

Until I found a voice, you had no way to know that I bear the cumulative sorrows of all who have ever died. Nevertheless, I resent the fact that for millennia I've been perceived as the villain in a scheme that adds to my own sadness as well as yours.

Try, at least, to grasp that I am not "the enemy of life"—far from it. We are symbiotic. Life cannot renew itself without me. Disease and accident may be life's enemies, but I am not; nor have I ever seen myself as yours.

I intensely dislike being—not the force, for I am the absence of a force—but the *fact* that thwarts your desire to live forever. Yet, I would be less than scrupulous if I did not try to help you align yourselves with the way things are: there is no immortality.

§

XVI

From the opening of this letter, I've referred to your lurid fantasies of me that have quickened mortal fears. I've suggested you think of me differently. Nonetheless, I suspect that the very concept of your own mortality remains incomprehensible to you. Since humans think with verbal images, you might try on this one. I find it closer than most ...

Life is channeled through you only briefly, yet *every* current is transient in its stream. You are related to all that has gone before you, all that will flow on. No less a part of nature are you than a wave that surges onto shore, only to be drawn back to the ocean. Why should you fear returning to the undifferentiated state from which you came? You do not seem to look *backward* in horror.

§

Life is channeled through you only briefly,
yet every current is transient
in its stream.

XVII

With equanimity you observe the deaths of
plants and animals as part of the self-perpetuating
cycle of life. For many of you, only the deaths of
human animals are seen as tragic. It is no wonder:
century after century certain religions and ideologies
have instructed you in this notion of the supremacy
of humans above all other living things. Finally, the
condition of the planet is mocking that fallacy.

The differences I detect between you and other
animals do not amount to superiority or inferiority.
To me, though, there is this stunning contrast—you
are storytellers, they are not.

The dying breaths of creatures deliver up to me
sensory memories more startlingly present than most
of yours. So immersed are they in their reality that
they record it with vivid alertness. They are not dis-
tracted by a perception of themselves as protago-
nists.   And unconcerned with the drama of a
personal saga, what reason would they have to

dread me?

By the time I meet your kind in adulthood, narrative memory has been working on your perceptions since you were two or three years old. Without being conscious of it then, you began to tell yourself your own story. Most of you are unaware of the continual revisions you make in order to maintain the sense—or the illusion, I would say—of a consistent self. I'm not critical of this. It is the way you hold yourself together.

You use narrative to explain yourself to yourself, as well as to explain yourselves to each other. I will allow that without your stories, I would have been less capable of understanding you. Complex emotions might never have taken hold in me without the rich and conflicting perspectives I've derived from your narratives.

You, of course, do not retain all the folklore, fairy tales, myths, legends, parables and personal stories that I do. But it could not hurt you to let a great sampling of them from disparate periods and cultures pass through you, to let them affect you, even change you. The only harm I see is if you cling too desperately to any. I need hardly remind you of the gripping narratives about me! Why should you feel pressed to do more than experience a story, to try it on and then let it go? You do not need to believe it in order to benefit from it.

You use stories to explain to children life and death—most often, as they were explained to you. The myths I learned from your forebears expressed childhood's magical ideas: that every event is willed by a sentient being, and that a parental gaze will be eternal. Myths and legends are second nature to you; yet you forget that, if it is a narrative at all, its origins are human.

Because your own lives begin and end, you try to apply this template to all of existence. From the creation tales told by shamans to the evolving narratives of science, you search for *the* beginning and ending. Why cannot there always have been *something*, changing now subtly, now explosively, but forever changing and evolving?

§

*The distortion of your original longing is
the one great human tragedy
from which so many others flow.*

XVIII

I had thought that closing this letter would be a relief to me. But, as I approach the end, I'm stirred by emotions only silence can reach.

I'll offer this last observation. To me, the distortion of your original longing—longing that is so beautiful in your infancy—is the one great human tragedy from which so many others flow.

I'm talking about the simple longing to be held, to be gazed at lovingly, to be nourished and filled. It is your common beginning. Why do you disregard it as your universal touchstone?

How can you not know how essential it is that these primal needs be filled at the beginning of every human life? For when such yearning is sorely unmet in its original simplicity, it mutates into a different kind of craving—for possessions, status, power—supremacy.

I know that the exquisite illusion of oneness with another person and with the world, which you experience so early, must inevitably shatter, for how could any of you achieve an independent existence otherwise?

How could you accept mortality if your earliest perceptions—so suggestive of immortality—were never broken? Yet I can attest that there remain subtle traces of your first disillusionment, wordless and profound, even in your final breaths.

I hold in high regard those of you who tenderly recall your most basic emotional needs, never failing to recognize that they exist in everyone, and so transform your original loss into compassion and empathy.

I will ask the rest of you the obvious question: Wouldn't it be more sane to realistically address the vulnerability you share on this earth than to devise more ways to kill and maim each other?

I have discovered from you that hope and faith can both grow out of longing. Hope does not require a leap away from careful observation of the world; faith too often does. For that reason, I cannot claim I have faith in humanity.

But—only because I know so intimately your underlying yearnings—I do have hope for you. Why would I have written this otherwise?

§

XIX

What I am about to do in ending this narrative is something like dying. I feel obliged to make an object lesson of myself, as all supernatural beings would do for you if they had your welfare in mind.

They would tell you honestly that they have no existence beyond human imagination. They would say to you, *Take care of one another, since I cannot, and live, live in this world, the only one you have.*

You do not need to have faith in me; you do not need to fear me. As you finish this letter, let us change places for a final moment ... there will be no more of me left *as persona* after these, my last words—I will exist only in what you may have taken in.

As ever,
Death

ACKNOWLEDGMENTS

The Letter from Death could not have been written without the critical input of my lifelong creative partner JP Somersaulter and my son Dave. They have been my sounding boards and editors from the idea stage forward. I have loved working with them, and I am grateful for Dave's commitment to illustrating the book even while living in London.

In order to inform Death's opinions, I've spent a great deal of time getting to the bottom of hell and other noxious destinations. Without the companionship of Pam Meiser, my tenacious and thorough research assistant, these might have been one-way trips.

This book is dedicated to Lilian Dreiser who, at ninety-two, has been one of my most intense and perceptive readers. Her advice and unflagging support have been a real force in the book's progression.

I 've learned something important from every one of my draft readers including Craig Berger, Janis Dees, Ming Fang He, Chris Hewlett, Kathleen McCrone, Michael Moats, Pam Meiser, Paula Moore and Bill Schubert, many of whom have consulted on each of my books. Happily, Pamela Livingston has found time in her demanding schedule to lend her editorial eye and hand once again.

Mary Bisbee-Beek has provided valuable coaching about bringing this book to the public, while making work decidedly more fun.

And finally, the support of my husband Michael and my sister Chris has gone beyond what one might expect of family. Both have shown unmistakable enthusiasm for this particular work, and this has sustained me. As one who has lived day-to-day with my pre-dictable self-doubts for tackling this taboo subject, Michael deserves my special thanks for his steadiness and conviction regarding the need for this book.

BIBLIOGRAPHY

The ideas that shaped *The Letter from Death* emerged from experiences and influences over decades, most of which I can no longer tease apart into separate strands. Death's voice has certainly been refined and informed, however, by my reading in recent years.

Among the authors below, I would like to thank two in particular whose books provided structure and content to which I could relate much of my other research. First, I highly recommend Alice Turner's *The History of Hell* (Harcourt, 1995) for its very readable scholarship and, frequently, its wit. While I used a wide variety of sources for Death's commentary on Hell, *The History of Hell* was the book I read first and the one to which I most often returned. As is true of any information gathered from my research for *The Letter from Death*, I take full responsibility for the selectivity and irony with which the character of Death deals with the material.

Likewise, in regard to *Science Goes to War* by Ernest Volkman (Wiley, 2002), Death's purposeful reductionism and biting tone is not reflective at all of Volkman's careful and compelling documentation, which I respect and commend. If any factual inaccuracies appear in *The Letter from Death*, they are unintentional and should not be attributed to any other author but me.

On Killing: the Psychological Cost of Learning to Kill in War and Society by Lt. Col. Dave Grossman (Little, Brown, 1995) also deserves special note. Though it could hardly be characterized as an anti-war book, it provides tough-minded insights about the responsibility society must accept for the culture of its military.

Grossman details the intensification of combat training that has occurred since U.S. Army Brigadier General S.L.A. Marshall's studies during World War II. These revealed the hidden aversion to killing that prevailed among soldiers. Grossman makes post-traumatic-stress disorder patently understandable. Just as importantly, he alerts us that, as a society, we are subjecting ourselves to a more dilute version of the kinds of conditioning that have caused such devastating contradictions in our soldiers.

The following books have also informed or influenced in some way the voice of Death.

Section II

Brandon, Samuel G. F. *The Personification of Death in Some Ancient Religions*. Manchester, England: The Librarian, The John Rylands Library, 1961.

"Cizin." *Encyclopædia Britannica Online*. http://www.search.eb.com/eb/article-9082772

Ellis, Peter Berresford. *A Dictionary of Irish Mythology*. Santa Barbara, CA: ABC-Clio, 1987.

Ferry, David. *Gilgamesh: A New Rendering in English Verse*. New York: Farrar, Straus, and Giroux, 1992.

Glasse, Cyril. *The New Encyclopedia of Islam*. Walnut Creek, CA: AltaMira Press, 2001.

Goring, Rosemary. *The Wordsworth Dictionary of Beliefs and Religions*. Ware: Wordsworth Editions, 1995.

"Hel." *Encyclopædia Britannica Online.* http://www.search.eb.com/eb/article-9039864

Herzberg, Max J. *Myths and Their Meaning*. Boston: Allyn and Bacon, 1960.

Holck, Frederick H. *Death and Eastern Thought: Understanding Death in Eastern Religions and Philosophies*. Nashville: Abingdon Press, 1974.

"'Izra'il." *Encyclopædia Britannica Online.* http://www.search.eb.com/eb/article-9043110

Jones, Lindsay. *Encyclopedia of Religion*. New York: Macmillan, 2005.

Katz, Brian P. *Deities and Demons of the Far East*. Myths of the World. New York: MetroBooks, 1995.

Lurker, Manfred. *The Routledge Dictionary of Gods, Goddesses, Devils and Demons*. London: Routledge, 2004.

Mercatante, Anthony S. and James R. Dow. *The Facts on File Encyclopedia of World Mythology and Legend*. Facts on file library of religion and mythology. New York: Facts on File, 2004.

"Morrigan." *Encyclopedia Mythica Online*.
http://www.pantheon.org/articles/m/morrigan.html

Netton, Ian Richard. *A Popular Dictionary of Islam*. Lincolnwood, Ill: NTC Pub. Group, 1997.

Orchard, Andy. *Dictionary of Norse Myth and Legend*. London: Cassell, 1997.

"Samael." *Jewish Encyclopedia Online*.
http://jewishencyclopedia.com

Skolnik, Fred, and Michael Berenbaum. *Encyclopaedia Judaica*. Detroit: Macmillan Reference USA, 2007.

Stutley, Margaret, and James Stutley. *Harper's Dictionary of Hinduism: Its Mythology, Folklore, Philosophy, Literature, and History*. San Francisco: Harper & Row, 1984.

Wigoder, Geoffrey, Fred Skolnik, and Shmuel Himelstein. *The New Encyclopedia of Judaism*. New York: New York University Press, 2002.

Williams, George M. *Handbook of Hindu Mythology*. Handbooks of World Mythology. Santa Barbara, Calif: ABC-CLIO, 2003.

"Yama." *Encyclopædia Britannica Online*.
http://www.search.eb.com/eb/article-9077752

Section V

Almond, Philip C. *Heaven and Hell in Enlightenment England*. Cambridge: Cambridge University Press, 1994.

Aries, Philippe. *The Hour of Our Death*. New York: Barnes & Noble, 2000.

Bernstein, Alan E. *The Formation of Hell: Death and Retribution in the Ancient and Early Christian Worlds*. Ithaca: Cornell University Press, 1993.

Camporesi, Piero. *The Fear of Hell: Images of Damnation and Salvation in Early Modern Europe*. University Park, PA: Pennsylvania State University Press, 1991.

Coulton, George G. *The Medieval Scene: An Informal Introduction to the Middle Ages*. Mineola, NY: Dover, 2000.

Delumeau, Jean. *Sin and Fear: The Emergence of a Western Guilt Culture, 13th-18th Centuries*. New York: St. Martin's Press, 1990.

Ehrman, Bart D. *God's Problem: How the Bible Fails to Answer Our Most Important Question—Why We Suffer*. New York: HarperOne, 2008.

Freud, Sigmund, James Strachey, and Peter Gay. *The Future of an Illusion*. New York: Norton, 1989.

Gardiner, Eileen. *Visions of Heaven and Hell before Dante*. New York: Italica Press, 1989.

Gibbs, Nancy. 2008. "The New Road to Hell." *Time*. 171, no. 12: 78.

Gurevic, Aron Jakovlevic. *Medieval Popular Culture: Problems of Belief and Perception*. Cambridge studies in oral and literate culture, 14. Cambridge: Cambridge University Press, 1988.

Huddleston, Gilbert. "Pope St. Gregory I ('the Great')." *The Catholic Encyclopedia Vol. 6*. New York: Robert Appleton Company, 1909. http://www.newadvent.org/cathen/06780a.htm

Hughes, Robert. *Heaven and Hell in Western Art*. New York: Stein and Day, 1968.

Jakapi, Roomet. "William Whiston, The Universal Deluge, and a Terrible Spectacle." *Electronic Journal of Folklore*. http://www.folklore.ee/folklore/vol31/jakapi.pdf

Mason, Stephen F. "Bishop John Wilkins, F.R.S. (1614-72): Analogies of Thought-Style in the Protestant Reformation and Early Modern Science." Notes and Records of the Royal Society of London 46, no. 1 (Jan., 1992): 1-21. http://www.jstor.org/stable/531438

Porter, Roy. *Flesh in the Age of Reason*. London: Allen Lane, 2003.

Quinsey, Vernon. *Book Reviews Summer 2003*. Queens University, Kingston, Ontario, Canada. http://psyc.queensu.ca/faculty/quinsey/borev03b. htm

"Seven Deadly Sins." *University of Leicester*. http://www.le.ac.uk/arthistory/seedcorn/ faq-sds.html

Soergel, Philip M. *Arts & Humanities Through the Eras. Renaissance Europe, 1300-1600*. Detroit: Thomson Gale, 2005.

Turner, Alice K. *The History of Hell*. San Diego: Harcourt Brace & Co, 1995.

Van Scott, Miriam. *Encyclopedia of Hell*. New York: St. Martin's Press, 1998.

Section VIII

Bellamy, Ronald F. 1992. "The Medical Effects of Conventional Weapons." *World Journal of Surgery*. 16, no. 5.

"Call to Nuclear Powers to Disarm." *BBC News*. http://news.bbc.co.uk/2/hi/americas/4504737.stm

Cernak, Ibolja, Jouan Savic, Dragan Ignjatovic, and Miodrag Jevtic. 1999. "Blast Injury from Explosive Munitions." *The Journal of Trauma*. 47, no. 1: 96-103.

Diagram Group. *Weapons: An International Encyclopedia from 5000 B.C. to 2000 A.D.* New York: St. Martin's Press, 1990.

Green, Robert. "Reflections on War: The Immediate and Long-term Effects of Modern Weapons." *Peace Movement Aotearoa.* http://www.converge.org.nz/pma/cra0989.htm

Hom, Gregory G. 2003. "Chemical, Biological, and Radiological Weapons: Implications for Optometry and Public Health." *Optometry: Journal of the American Optometric Association.* 74, no. 2: 81.

Kadivar, Hooshang and Stephen C. Adams. 1991. "Treatment of Chemical and Biological Warfare Injuries: Insights Derived from the 1984 Iraqi Attack on Majnoon Island." *Military Medicine.* 156, no. 4: 171-7.

Kasthuri A.S., A.B. Pradhan, S.K. Dham, I.P. Bhalla, and J.S. Paul. 1990. "Nuclear, Biological and Chemical Warfare. Part I: Medical Aspects of Nuclear Warfare." *The Journal of the Association of Physicians of India.* 38, no. 4: 292-4.

Knudson Gregory B., et al. 2002. "Nuclear, Biological, and Chemical Combined Injuries and Countermeasures on the Battlefield." *Military Medicine.* 167, no. 2: 95-7.

Norris, Robert S. and Hans M. Kristensen. "New Estimates of the U.S. Nuclear Weapons Stockpile, 2007

and 2012." *Issues: Nuclear Weapons, Waste & Energy*.
http://www.nrdc.org/nuclear/stockpile_2007-
2012.asp

Norris, Robert S. and Hans M. Kristensen. "U.S. Nuclear
Forces, 2008." *Bulletin of the Atomic Scientists*. 64,
no. 1: 50.

Peters, Ann. 1996. "Blinding Laser Weapons." *Medicine,
Conflict, and Survival*. 12, no. 2: 107-113.

"Precision-guided munitions." *Wikipedia*.
http://en.wikipedia.org/wiki/Precision-guided_
munition

Sharkey, Noel. 2007. "Automated Killers and the Com-
puting Profession." *Computer*. 40, no. 11: 124.

"Table of Global Nuclear Weapons Stockpile, 1945-
2002." *Natural Resources Defense Council*.
http://www.nrdc.org/nuclear/nudb/datab19.asp

Volkman, Ernest. *Science Goes to War: The Search for
the Ultimate Weapon, from Greek Fire to Star Wars*.
New York: Wiley, 2002.

Wiedeman, James E. 1994. "Rocket Grenade Injuries:
Patient Management in a Field Hospital Setting."
Military Medicine. 159, no. 1: 77-9.

Section X

Berman, Morris. *Wandering God: A Study in Nomadic Spirituality*. Albany: State University of New York Press, 2000.

Chomsky, Noam. *Media Control: The Spectacular Achievements of Propaganda*. New York: Seven Stories Press, 1997.

Fry, Douglas P. *The Human Potential for Peace: An Anthropological Challenge to Assumptions About War and Violence*. New York: Oxford University Press, 2006.

Gray, John. *Straw Dogs: Thoughts on Humans and Other Animals*. London: Granta, 2002.

Grossman, Dave. *On Killing: The Psychological Cost of Learning to Kill in War and Society*. Boston: Little, Brown, 1995.

Herman, Edward S. and Noam Chomsky. *Manufacturing Consent: The Political Economy of the Mass Media*. New York: Pantheon Books, 2002.

Kemp, Graham, and Douglas P. Fry. *Keeping the Peace: Conflict Resolution and Peaceful Societies Around the World*. New York: Routledge, 2004.

Mansfield, Sue. *The Gestalts of War: An Inquiry into Its Origins and Meanings As a Social Institution*. New York: Dial Press, 1982.

Regal, Philip J. *The Anatomy of Judgment*. Minneapolis: University of Minnesota Press, 1990.

Sharp, Gene. *From Dictatorship to Democracy: A Conceptual Framework for Liberation*. East Boston, MA: The Albert Einstein Institution, 2008.

Sharp, Gene. *Making the Abolition of War a Realistic Goal*. New York: Sponsored by Institute for World Order, 1980.

Sharp, Gene, and Joshua Paulson. *Waging Nonviolent Struggle: 20th Century Practice and 21st Century Potential*. Boston: Extending Horizons Books, 2005.

Swanbrow, Diane. "Vicious Videos." *Michigan Today*, Summer 2006, 8-11.

Waal, F. B. M. de. *Our Inner Ape: A Leading Primatologist Explains Why We Are Who We Are*. New York: Riverhead Books, 2005.

Waal, F. B. M. de. *Peacemaking Among Primates*. Cambridge, Mass: Harvard University Press, 1989.

Waal, F. B. M. de, and Frans Lanting. *Bonobo: The Forgotten Ape*. Berkeley: University of California Press, 1997.

Watson, Peter. *War on the Mind: The Military Uses and Abuses of Psychology*. New York: Basic Books, 1978.

Zimbardo, Philip G. *The Lucifer Effect: Understanding How Good People Turn Evil*. New York: Random House, 2007.

Zinn, Howard. *Artists in Times of War*. New York: Seven Stories Press, 2003.

Zinn, Howard. *The Power of Nonviolence: Writings by Advocates of Peace*. Boston: Beacon Press, 2002.

Zinn, Howard. *The Twentieth Century: A People's History*. New York: Perennial, 2003.

Other

Anouilh, Jean, and Lewis Galantiere. *Antigone: A Tragedy*. Methuen modern plays. London: Methuen Drama, 2000.

Brown, Lester Russell. *Plan B 2.0: Rescuing a Planet Under Stress and a Civilization in Trouble*. New York: W.W. Norton & Co, 2006.

Cameron, Kenneth Neill. "Life, Death and Purpose." in *Dialectical Materialism and Modern Science*. New York: International Publishers, 1995.

Capra, Fritjof. *The Web of Life: A New Scientific Understanding of Living Systems*. New York: Anchor Books, 1996.

Damasio, Antonio R. *The Feeling of What Happens: Body and Emotion in the Making of Consciousness*. New York: Harcourt Brace, 1999.

Didion, Joan. *The Year of Magical Thinking*. New York: A.A. Knopf, 2005.

Hawken, Paul. *Blessed Unrest: How the Largest Movement in the World Came into Being, and Why No One Saw It Coming*. New York: Viking, 2007.

Hawken, Paul. *The Ecology of Commerce: A Declaration of Sustainability*. New York: HarperBusiness, 1993.

Nuland, Sherwin B. *How We Die: Reflections on Life's Final Chapter*. New York: Vintage Books, 1995.

Siegel, Daniel J. *The Developing Mind: Toward a Neurobiology of Interpersonal Experience*. New York: Guilford Press, 1999.

Smith, Bradford. *Dear Gift of Life; A Man's Encounter with Death*. Wallingford, Pa: Pendle Hill Pub, 1965.

Stern, Daniel N. *The Interpersonal World of the Infant: A View from Psychoanalysis and Developmental Psychology*. New York: Basic Books, 1985.

Worldwatch Institute. *State of the World 2006: A Worldwatch Institute Report on Progress Toward a Sustainable Society*. New York: W.W. Norton, 2006.